GAY ROMANCE COLLECTION

CONNOR WHITELEY

No part of this book may be reproduced in any form or by any electronic or mechanical means. Including information storage, and retrieval systems, without written permission from the author except for the use of brief quotations in a book review.

This book is NOT legal, professional, medical, financial or any type of official advice.

Any questions about the book, rights licensing, or to contact the author, please email connorwhiteley@connorwhiteley.net

Copyright © 2021 CONNOR WHITELEY

All rights reserved.

DEDICATION
Thank you to all my readers without you I couldn't do what I love.

ROUND THE PARK AND BEYOND

Feeling the cold wooden floor of his London apartment, Charlie let out a long breath as he placed the final cardboard box filled with bits and pieces on top of the other boxes. The cardboard felt cold and smooth as he ran his fingers over them. So many memories and so much stuff.

Turning around, Charlie gave a half smile as he looked at the rest of his apartment. It was a simple but fairly expensive apartment in the heart of wonderful London. The large room was easily large enough to fit fifty people in with its long smooth white walls and high ceiling.

One of Charlie's favourite features had to be the great design of it all. He had a large living room with two sofas in the front, a small bedroom to the side in another room and a massive kitchen and entertainment space in the back.

Some people said it was open concept taken to

the extreme, but he liked it. It allowed him to have some great parties and entertain friends and family when they came. And everyone was impressed the walls of the apartment stopped the noisy London city traffic and trains from getting into the apartment.

Charlie knew what that was like. Studying at university in London was a nightmare when you lived near a main road. So much traffic at all hours of the night. But here in this apartment, you had no idea you were in noisy London.

But it also opened his heart open to such pain and agony.

Charlie only had to smell the air with its sweet earthy, manly aftershave to be reminded of that fact. His boyfriend of five whole years had walked out on him last week. The jerk. Five whole years wasted. He couldn't even bring himself to say his ex's name.

Charlie frowned as he thought about the stupid mistake of letting him talk Charlie into moving to Durham in the far North for his new job.

Of course, at the time it sounded great, Charlie had always wanted to move away from London. He wanted to go and experience the world and Durham sounded like the right start. Then maybe Scotland, and maybe outside the United Kingdom.

Charlie cupped his face with his smooth hands as he remembered how as soon as Charlie had given notice at work and sorted out the buyers for the apartment. That ex had left him.

He really didn't want to tell his friends and

family. They all said the ex was a nightmare and Charlie was better off without him. But Charlie loved him. He thought the ex loved him back.

Turning his attention back to the pile of cardboard boxes Charlie knew he hated this. In the space of a week, he had lost the love of his life and his favourite apartment.

It wouldn't be long until the moving company came and helped Charlie move his stuff. Looking at all the boxes filled with his memories and things from his life. Charlie felt so empty. This was all so pointless. How could someone's life be boxed up so perfectly and moved?

He supposed the only positive of this entire thing was Charlie had managed to convince his hot friend Chris (sadly straight) to let him stay with him in Durham for a month or two. Whilst Charlie got himself sorted.

Charlie wanted to scream at the thought of having to depend on the charity from others to survive. He had tried so hard to be his own person and support himself. But Charlie supposed he didn't think his ex would abandon him. He probably wasn't even going to Durham for work but Charlie just wanted to leave London and get away from all of this.

He especially didn't want to see the buyers of *his* apartment and he definitely didn't want to see his ex if he was still in London.

Listening to the noisy traffic outside and what sounded like lots of different people shouting at each other. Charlie really wanted to escape for a few hours. So he needed to go to the only place he could relax: Russell Park.

***

It was amazing that such a wonderful place existed in London. Which Kieran guessed was why he loved it here.

Looking at the thick rows of trees and wild plants that boarded the park and the busy streets of London was brilliant. Kieran could hear the squirrels climbing up and down the trees and the birds singing.

A perfect escape from chaotic London.

Looking at the amazing park, Kieran loved everything about it from the little ring pathway in front of the row of trees outlining the park. To the large café and different pieces of entertainment in the middle.

Or to be honest, Kieran had to admit he loved the natural part of Russell Park. Turning to his left he walked towards one of the two massive bug hotels in the park.

Where some people would see an ugly pile of wooden logs in front of a wooden hotel thing, Kieran saw nature at its finest. The large wooden hotel thing was divided into five sections filled with different things for the bugs and butterflies to enjoy. From rough pinecones to the twigs and more.

Kieran knew it was great London was trying to protect wildlife and give Londoners a piece of greenery. And Kieran did love all the clever tricks

Russell Park used to protect and conserve nature. From the obvious bug hotels to the fenced off patches of long bright green grass. That allowed the bugs and other creatures to nest safely.

Smelling the bitter coffee mixed with the smell of the fresh trees, Kieran made a note to go and get a massive cup of coffee from the café later on. They did make some great coffee and pastries too.

The sound of birds singing, people talking and children running and laughing reminded Kieran of why he loved this place. It was like a little oasis in the middle of a desert.

As much as Kieran loved London and Russell Park, he didn't like the constant traffic and rush of the city. But here in the park, it was different. A little bit of peace. A break from the rush of city life.

With the smell of hot bitter coffee returning to his nose and the taste of bitter chocolatey notes forming on his tongue, Kieran started to turn away from the bug hotel. He needed some of that hot coffee.

But as he turned, he stopped.

The sound of footsteps made him smile as Kieran looked at the stunning stranger walking into the park. His smooth youthful skin was perfect. His beautiful face angular and soft. The Stranger's longish brown hair blew slightly in the warm wind, and it looked perfect. (As did the Stranger's body. He was fit.)

The Stranger looked sad but then he seemed to

relax and all the tension left his body as he entered the park and breathed in the fresh park air.

Kieran couldn't blame him. He always came here from work to destress, but he had never seen this beautiful Stranger before.

Then Kieran only realised his foot and body had continued to walk towards this beautiful Stranger without his brain telling him to.

A part of Kieran wanted to kick himself at this, he wasn't a weirdo who randomly walked up to every man he liked. He would probably be arrested if he did that. But The Stranger was beautiful. Kieran wouldn't mind running his fingers through The Stranger's stunning hair.

What was wrong with Kieran? He never acted like this, Kieran really wanted to kick or pinch himself now. He needed to act normal.

But his body had got himself into this situation. What could he do? Walk away? No that would be too weird.

The Stranger gave Kieran a stunning smile and he couldn't help but give him one back. His stomach churned and danced at the sight of that stunning smile.

Kieran's smile deepened as he realised that he needed to talk to The Stranger. But Kieran definitely had a good feeling about this.

***

Feeling the slightly warm tarmac footpath as he stepped into the park, Charlie could feel all his tension leave him. All his problems and the tread that filled him just went away. He knew this was going to be a great few hours. For a change, he could forget about the move and just focus on himself and the beautiful park.

Admiring the utterly stunning border of thick trees and wild nature that separated the fence of the park with the ring footpath going around the entire beautiful park. Charlie smiled (the first time in a while) as he listened to the birds singing away and the squirrels hurrying up and down the trees.

Of course after his last encounter of almost getting chased by squirrels, Charlie was going to stay well away from them. He didn't want to be chased today.

Feeling the warmish sun beam down on him through the trees, a part of Charlie just wondered what he should do. Should he just walk around like a lost pup? Sit at the large, pleasant café in the middle of the park by himself? No.

A part of Charlie would love to go and sit in the café. All that bitter smelling coffee with their amazing pastries and other delights smelt great. The atmosphere was welcoming and it provided a perfect break from the city.

But that had been where Charlie and his ex loved to go. He couldn't go in there. What if people asked about his ex? Or worse, what if his ex was in there?

Maybe this had been a mistake. Maybe Charlie should leave London and never return.

About to turn around something caught Charlie's eye. Looking over by the large bug hotel, Charlie gave a massive smile as he saw an utterly stunning Mystery Guy.

He had never seen this Guy before but he was perfect. His hair was short and it blew slightly in the breeze and the Guy's perfect strong jawline and his muscles looked perfect.

Then the Mystery Guy turned and smiled at Charlie, and (Charlie couldn't believe it) the Mystery Guy was walking over.

This didn't happen to him. Charlie didn't get the attention of all the hot guys. Normally other people had to introduce him. Hot guys never paid attention to him.

Charlie was half attempt to turn around to check if there was a fellow hot guy behind him. But Mystery Guy was definitely staring and smiling at him.

Well, Charlie had to admit this Mystery Guy was stunning. His smile was like a movie star. No, this Guy had to be mistaken. There had to be someone else behind him.

Then Charlie's heart skipped a few beats as the Mystery Guy stopped in front of him and smiled. This wasn't happening.

Even better (or worse) the Mystery Guy held out his hand. Charlie couldn't shake his hand. They had only just met. What if Charlie's handshake was poor? What if Mystery Guy thought Charlie was silly and weak? You could tell a lot from a handshake.

"I don't bite," the Mystery Guy said, his voice beautifully smooth and manly.

Charlie's smile grew.

Then Charlie wanted to kick himself. Now the Mystery Guy knew Charlie was nervous. That was bad. Why was Charlie acting like this? At work he was a calm, collective man. He wasn't that today.

Charlie shook Mystery's Guy smooth velvety hand. Charlie's stomach flipped and butterflies went crazy as he loved the feel of Mystery's Guy soft skin.

"Kieran," the Mystery Guy said. Charlie must have looked confused. "My name,"

Kieran.

That was a hot name. Perfect for this Guy.

"Charlie," he said.

Kieran smiled at hearing his name. Did he like it? What if Charlie was a bad name? It was nowhere near as sexy as *Kieran.*

"I haven't seen you before," Kieran said, his voice beautiful.

"I normally come in the evening, weekends, sometimes lunch. You?" Charlie asked.

"Every afternoon. I love it here. It's perfect. Especially today,"

Charlie smiled a little more. (As if that was possible)

"Charlie," Kieran said.

Charlie smiled as Kieran said it wonderfully and seductively.

"You looked a little sad when I saw you. Are you

okay?" Kieran asked.

Now that was just typical. Charlie's stomach churned as he wondered how he wasn't going to mess this up. If this jerk of an ex hadn't messed up his life anymore. Now his ex was going to mess up this. A perfectly beautiful guy who actually seemed to care about him was going to learn about how messed up his life was. Charlie was hardly impressed.

What could he do? Lie? Dodge the question?

If his mother or father was here (not that they would approve of any man for Charlie) they would probably get him to tell the truth. They were right about his jerk of an ex after all. Maybe Charlie should have trusted them then, maybe he would trust them now.

"Um, I don't want to burden you," Charlie said.

Kieran gently touched his arm. Electricity ran up Charlie's arm. (and to other wayward organs)

"It's no trouble. I want to hear it," Kieran said.

Charlie smiled as he saw Kieran look to the floor as he probably realised, he sounded like he cared a bit too much.

"It's my ex. He left me,"

Kieran looked like he felt bad for asking.

"It's fine. But we were going to move to Durham together for his job. My apartment's sold and I'll be moving. Oh I don't know,"

Kieran stroked Charlie's arm.

Charlie really wanted this perfect beautiful man to do more. He wanted more comfort but Charlie knew not to get too far ahead. Why was he even unloading his problems onto this guy?

Kieran smiled. "Durham?"

"Yea,"

"It's just I have a little holiday home there,"

Charlie didn't know where to be delighted or not. This beautiful perfect man had a place where he was going. But no, no, no this couldn't happen. Charlie didn't want to be hurt again.

He just wanted to go away from London. He was already going to stay with Chris in Durham while he got his life back on track.

Charlie opened his mouth.

"I'm sorry I shouldn't have said anything," Kieran said.

"Walk with me," Charlie said.

***

Kieran wasn't entirely sure whether or not to follow Charlie as he started to walk along the long yellow ring footpath around the park. With the wonderful thick trees and wild plants on one side and the thick lustrous green grass on the other.

The birds continued to sing, and the people and children kept laughing in the warmish afternoon sun.

Kieran had to pause for a moment. Should he really walk with Charlie? After all his ex-boyfriend had just broken up with him. What if Charlie only wanted to walk with him for some weird kind of rebound?

Looking ahead, Kieran admired beautiful Charlie as he confidently walked along the footpath. His steps strong and confident. He clearly didn't care if people saw them.

That always was one of Kieran's flaws. He was never really sold on the idea of public displays of affection with other boys. Was Kieran just being silly?

Usually, he never panicked or thought before acting. But this time it was different. This time he was hesitant. Kieran didn't want to make a mistake. Why was he acting like such a teenager?

Like Kieran, Charlie must have walked round this park with boys before. It was a great spot to walk, catch up and even kiss in public.

No one ever minded here. Everyone was here for the little piece of the oasis amongst chaotic London.

The smell of sweet, bitter coffee mixed with the refreshing scent of the trees filled Kieran's nose.

A part of Kieran just really wanted to be with Charlie but this boy he had met ten minutes ago was in such pain surely. He didn't want what he needed. Should Kieran really enter that? He didn't know. He didn't want to make it worse. If anything Kieran wanted to help Charlie and make his life better.

Then there was where Charlie's life was taking him. To Durham. Too far, far away from London. Maybe Charlie did want a fresh start away from everything. Surely, Kieran would be trespassing on this new life.

Knowing he was being silly and pointless, Kieran knew he had to walk with Charlie. He was beautiful and Kieran hadn't acted or thought like this ever. He felt happy, relaxed and his stomach churned and danced at the thought of Charlie.

As soon as they shook hands, Kieran had felt the power and chemistry between them. he really wanted to be with Charlie. And so what if Charlie's life was going in a strange direction, wouldn't it be good if Charlie had someone to support him?

Kieran nodded. He needed to walk with Charlie maybe just around the park but maybe beyond.

***

Feeling the slightly warm yellow tarmac of the yellow ring footpath beneath his feet as he walked. His heart raced and panicked as he thought that Kieran might not walk with him. Charlie needed him. He wanted to get to know him.

Kieran was stunning. His perfect face and face. Even the thought of Kieran made blood rush to certain places.

Admiring a massive tree as he walked past, Charlie admitted this park was beautiful. The wonderful row or border of thick trees was great. It was the perfect reminder of an escape within the chaos of a big city.

Maybe Charlie would miss it. But why did he have to leave? Maybe Kieran had a place!

He tried to force the thoughts out of his mind. That was unfair. That was really unfair. Considering Kieran wasn't even walking with him. Maybe it was a sign.

Charlie frowned at the thought at Kieran not

wanting to be with him. He knew it was silly. He had just met Kieran but it was like one of those crazy love films you hear about. When Charlie was with Kieran he felt great, he felt alive and happy. He wanted that feeling. Charlie wanted to feel happiness every day.

A part of Charlie wanted to turn around and shake Kieran's hand once more. (And do more of course) Charlie just wanted to feel that smooth perfect skin one more time and look into those amazing eyes.

Charlie didn't know what he was going to do next with his life but he knew for a fact he wanted Kieran with him. He wanted, no needed a strong beautiful person by his side.

Taking a deep breath and smelling all the strong bitter coffee and the arguably pleasant smell of trees, Charlie thought about the horrible reality he faced when he went back to his apartment. The moving people would be there. Then he would have to return to real life. And get off his romantic high.

Charlie felt someone hold his hand. He recognised those wonderfully smooth, perfect hand and fingers. It was Kieran.

"I'll walk with you," Kieran said, his voice amazing.

Charlie didn't care. He kissed Kieran and now he really didn't care what would happen in his life now. He had Kieran. He had a strong beautiful man at his side who actually cared about him.

As they walked round the park, Charlie knew this

was going to be a great walk and hopefully beyond.

HEART AROUND THE STONES

Feeling the soft brown mud under his feet as he walked, William smiled as he looked in wonder at the natural beauty around him. As he continued to walk on the trail in the south west of England, William knew this was going to be a great day.

Admiring the trees and small green bushes lining each edge of the trail and the flat large green fields beyond, this was beautiful. The footpath to Stonehenge was stunning.

Some people said it was a long walk, but William loved that. He loved being out in the open English countryside. The air smelt so clean and fresh compared to the horrible dirty air of London and the other British cities.

But William had to admit Edinburg and Glasgow were great cities. Their air was fairly fresh too.

Hearing the large minibuses travelling up and down the road behind the trees and bushes, William shook his head. Of course he didn't have anything against these people by if you're going to go to Stonehenge then you need to experience it all. Including the long walk through the stunning countryside.

Looking up William smiled at the sight of the bright vibrant tree leaves and the bright blue sky above. The weather was perfect. It was going to be a great day.

He had been meaning to come here for years. Especially when him and his ex-boyfriend had decided to do some backpacking across the south of England. From the beautiful coastline of Kent to the historical and interesting counties of Devon and Cornwall.

So many great memories of the food, the fresh air, the history but most of all the freedom to explore the country they lived in (and each other!).

Then William frowned as he remembered what came next. They got back to London and their corporate jobs. William an accountant and his ex an employment lawyer. London was hardly short of work.

William's eyes widened as he stepped into a large muddy puddle and the cold refreshing water went up to his ankle. That's why he always wore hiking boots when he was out.

Returning to his train of thought, William knew he was happiest when not in London. The cold climate, the traffic, the noise, the pollution. It sucked the life out of him (and not the way he liked it)

Breathing in the wonderful fresh air, William didn't regret his choice to leave London and his boyfriend to a life of moving. But a life in the countryside and naturally William had found it difficult at first. He didn't like leaving his friends and family in London and Kent. But he did this for himself. He needed a new life for adventure, clean air and... William wanted to think of love yet that seemed like a silly idea.

Going up a slight hill the mud continued to move under his boots making him slip and slide. That's what was fun about the countryside. How each and every walk or going out could be made into a simple adventure just because of the weather.

Sadly, that's what his ex could never understand. A part of William knew his ex-boyfriend had missed out something great. But William couldn't wait for his adventure to begin and today he was going to visit a wonderful place he had always wanted to go.

***

Looking around over the utterly amazing and beautiful flat green fields of Stonehenge, Luke couldn't help but smile. This was amazing. He was actually at Stonehenge!

The land was so flat here with thick beautiful trees growing in between the fields with massive stretches of land left to nature. It was incredible!

And Luke couldn't believe the sweet refreshing smell of the air, it was actually clean. It wasn't polluted. It was how air was meant to be. He was surprised the taste of pine formed on his tongue.

With the bright sun in the crystal clean blue sky beaming down on Luke, he couldn't believe how brilliant this day was going to be. For the past two weeks there was nothing but constant rain but today it was perfectly sunny.

Feeling the hot sun against the back of his neck, Luke wanted to continue to admire the stunning countryside and its massive fields for a few moments longer. But Luke knew he had to look at the mighty Stonehenge.

Luke didn't want to look just yet. After all this was so beautiful and perfect, the closest Luke had come to seeing land like this was in movies. He didn't really see this in the city of London. Sure there were the old parks, St James Park, Russell Park and the others. But they were still in a horrible, polluted city. This nature beauty was in a league of its own.

At last he decided to slowly turn around and admire the mighty and all powerful Stonehenge. He had heard so much about it through TV, books and movies but this was stunning and these utterly failed to capture its beauty.

In front of him was a truly massive stone circle made up of large grey stone blocks in a simple circle shape. One half of the circle was more complete than the other but it was amazing.

The stone blocks looked surprisingly smooth for its age of well over 2,000 years old. It was just amazing how things could last this long. The history of this place was full of mystery and myths. That's what made it so amazing.

Luke's eyes narrowed as he focused on every little detail of the massive grey stone blocks and the signs of ageing were minimal. Sure he knew a few stones had fallen over during its long life but it was still impressive.

Walking up as far as he could before the waist hight rope stopped him, Luke really didn't want to leave and at least he had a few hours left to admire it.

The artist part of him wished he had bought his camera equipment and maybe even his drawing pencils and crayons. But Luke smiled as he thought about the hard lessons he had learnt about that in the past. It was always best to go to a location first, see what it was like and then decide if taking the equipment was needed.

Thankfully, Luke had met a (hot) guy earlier who was also an artist and he had said him and his wife (shame) the best time for artists in early morning or lunch time on weekdays. Considering it was a Saturday early afternoon, Luke knew he might need to return soon.

Something out of the corner of Luke's eye caught his attention. Thinking it was nothing Luke turned slightly and... wow!

There was an utterly stunning guy a few metres from him. That very short brown hair was cut perfectly and his strong muscles under his black sportwear t-shirts (very sensible) and his entire body just spoke of confidence and being extremely fit. Judging by the hiking boots Luke knew this Hiker had walked up here.

Luke would have smiled at that alone. He had seen the route here and how long it was. That was some hike so the fact Hiker had enough determination and fitness to do it that was even more appealing.

Luke couldn't stop smiling at the Hiker. He was perfect, fit and he looked great. Then it dawned on Luke he needed to stop staring. He didn't want people to think he was a crept. Luke was a perfectly normal guy. Except the butterflies in his stomach said otherwise.

The teenager part of Luke wondered what the Hiker's name was. Him and his friends loved playing that game. Luke decided it had to be a hot name like Harry, Kieran or maybe William. Luke really wanted it to be a hot name.

But as Luke kept smiling at the Hiker and looking at his beautiful face, Luke didn't care what the name was. The Hiker was beautiful.

Then it dawned on Luke, the Hiker was staring at him too.

***

William had to stop as he saw the majesty and beauty of Stonehenge. It was breath-taking and the walk had made it an even greater sight. A small part of William wanted to tell everyone who got the minibus up here what they were missing. But maybe that would be his little secret. The long walk through all the soft mud and refreshing air had definitely made the sight of Stonehenge worth it.

Staring at the immense chunks of grey stone blocks in the circle with some making big stone archways and some stone blocks fallen over and many more standing up. William couldn't believe that this was made thousands of years ago. It was a great achievement and the walk definitely helped. It was amazing. Simply amazing.

Now he was here, William felt the warm gentle breeze smelling refreshing and clean air blowing across the open fields and the hot sun beam down on him. Perfect weather for admiring something so amazing.

The sound of people chatting and the wind blowing was almost a reward in itself as William stood there with everyone admiring the same thing. Of course he was one of the few that walked through the breath-taking countryside to get here, but William didn't mind.

William was about to admire the stone blocks when he saw someone looking at him. A part of William thought it might be a weirdo or some crept. The amount of them he had to deal with back in the London gay bars were unreal.

Then looking at the Staring Guy, William instantly smiled. Staring Guy was hot. The hottest person William had seen for ages. Definitely since moving down here.

Staring Guy's face was smooth, youthful and squarish. His longish stunning brown hair looked amazing in the sunlight. William really wanted to run his fingers through that perfect soft looking hair.

Even Staring Guy's smile was breath-taking as he revealed his perfect pearly white teeth. Wow. Just wow.

William wanted to look away but he couldn't. Staring Guy was just too beautiful. Then a small part of him wanted to kick himself because he never did this. William wasn't the type of guy who stared constantly like a teenage boy at others. He was a confident and showed interest in boys in subtle ways. He wasn't the staring type.

Noticing his hands were sweaty and his heart was going a little faster, William wanted to say it was the long walk here that caused it. But he knew it was this beautiful boy in front of him.

But what should William do? He didn't want to be pointlessly looking at Staring Guy. What if someone thought it was weird? Eve worse, what if Staring Guy thought it was weird and didn't want to talk to him?

Then it looked as if Staring Guy realised William was looking at him and both their smiles deepened. As his stomach did flips and his hands sweated a little more, William knew this was going to be good.

He really hoped he wouldn't blow it.

"Hey," William said, instantly regretting it. That was a silly first thing to say.

Staring Guy smiled and almost seemed to laugh.

"Hi, I'm Luke,"

William's stomach did little backflips and the butterflies within him went crazy. *Luke*. That was a great name, it sounded great on the tongue.

"William," he said.

Luke gave William a boyish smile. Did he like the name? William wondered if his name was off putting.

It was a strange name. It was... William forced himself to concentrate back on beautiful Luke. It wasn't hard.

"You walked?" Luke asked.

"Yea, the walking is amazing. Have you done it?"

Luke shook his head and quietly said "No,"

"Oh it's amazing. We have to do it. You get to see so much on the way back. It's amazing,"

William realised he must have sounded like a desperate teenager by his excitement but at least Luke gave him a small laugh, his laugh was cute, sexy and hot.

"I'll think about it. You local?" Luke asked.

"Yea just moved here recently. You?"

"On holiday for the week *alone*,"

A part of William went sad at hearing Luke was only here for a week. It meant only a week to see him before he went on his way and lived his life. All whilst William stayed here alone and unloved. Really? He hated himself for thinking like this. He only just met *Luke* but he was so beautiful.

"You been here before," Luke asked.

"Na always wanted to come here. Only came because I'm single. Boyfriend didn't want to come here," William said.

Luke smiled and nodded.

The sensible part of William really wanted to kick himself. He never acted like this. He never wanted to drop (not so) subtle hints about his availability to a hot guy.

"What time you heading back?" Luke asked.

William cocked his head unsure of what Luke was implying but he understood after a few seconds.

"About an hour," William said.

"Meet back here then, and you can show me the breath-taking view on the walk,"

William smiled.

"Um if you want. If not it's totally cool if you don't," Luke said.

William almost laughed. At least he wasn't the only one struggling to act normal. He wanted to act cool so William simply said:

"Sure, see you in an hour,"

Luke smiled and started to walk away. He kept looking back with a massive boyish grin on his face.

William couldn't stop smiling too. He really wanted this hour to go quickly.

***

As the hour slowly counted down, Luke couldn't stop himself smiling as he replayed the encounter with the sexy, stunning *William* over and over in his mind.

Whilst the artist side of him wanted to admire and focus on the massive grey stone blocks in front of him. With some fallen over, some forming stone archways and others standing high into the sky. And listen to the conversations all the different people were having around him. The other part of Luke wanted to only think about the stunning William.

Breathing in the fresh cool air that smelt of nature, Luke couldn't deny William was just amazing. That sexy voice, his fitness, just everything was amazing about him.

Feeling the cool air gently blow across his face, Luke checked the time and thankfully there was only fifthteen minutes left. It was a shame. Luke just wanted to be with William and not looking at some stones. The stones were beautiful in their own right but they weren't William beautiful. His stomach filled with butterflies at the thought.

Luke smiled as he thought about William's name. It was a hot name and the person was even hotter than the name sounded.

Thinking about his holiday, the butterflies in his stomach calmed down a little bit as Luke thought about his holiday. He was only here for another week then he would have to return to London. That noisy, polluted place with all the traffic. But life was so simple and beautiful out here in the country.

There weren't any of the normal concerns like what time to catch the Tube, where was the nearest black cab and everything thing that comes with London. But most importantly William was here. A hot, beautiful guy who loved the countryside.

A small piece of Luke knew he needed to go back to London, his job and all his friends were there. Yet he could make friends again and there were these things called phones nowadays. Luke could just text and phone them. He just needed William.

Looking back at the stunning massive stone chunks of Stonehenge with the warmish late afternoon sun shining down on him, Luke tried to see himself living here in the countryside.

Then he simply smiled because it wouldn't be hard. It would be great since this countryside didn't have all the problems and difficulties London and other big cities had. This was a perfect countryside area (hopefully) with the amazing hot William by his side.

Checking the time a final time, Luke gave a massive smile as he realise it was almost time, it was almost time to walk back with William. Luke had walked his heart around the stones so now it was time to walk back with William.

***

Feeling the soft mud under his feet, William looked away from the massive blocks of amazing grey stone as he admired the wonderful, breath-taking open grass fields around Stonehenge. This was why he loved the countryside. It gave him access to all this wonderful nature, something he never ever could have imagined seeing in London.

Breathing in the stunning refreshing crisp air, William hoped Luke would turn up. Luke was adorable and so stunning. He was even more beautiful and amazing than all this nature. William really wanted to run his fingers through Luke's long brown hair.

The part of him earlier that wanted to kick himself for acting like a teenager was gone. William didn't care about acting like a fool he really cared about Luke. This was the first time since breaking up with his ex that he felt happy, alive and excited.

Feeling the cool late afternoon air blow past him, William's hands weren't sweaty anymore but his stomach still did little flips of excitement about walking back with Luke. It could be the start of something amazing. Of course that's if Luke showed up. William wanted him to so bad.

Hearing people laugh, kiss and chat as they left on the minibus, William gave them all a devilish smile as he knew if Luke came they would probably have the walking route to themselves. They would be able to experience the stunning walk back in peace.

But William still wasn't sure what would happen next. He was scared. William had been in this situation before, loving a really, really hot guy that dumped you the second things changed. William didn't want that to happen again, could things be different with Luke?

He wasn't sure but he wanted to take a risk. Luke seemed exactly the kind of hot, kind wonderful guy that a person should take a risk for. And a memory of William's mother popped into his mind telling him to take risks because you don't want to regret things in life. Whilst he wasn't exactly keen on his mother, she might be right in this case.

Wanting to turn around to see if Luke was behind him, William's hands turned sweaty and he took a deep refreshing breath as he slowly turned around.

Thankfully Luke with his beautiful face and longish brown hair was standing behind him. They both smiled at each other. William couldn't believe his luck, this beautiful boy wanted to walk back with him. He ran his fingers through Luke's perfect soft long hair. They both stared for a moment into each other's eyes.

Holding each other's hand as they started to walk back with the soft mud moving under their feet. William knew this was going to be a great walk back and definitely a great week, and hopefully a lot, lot longer.

MEMORABLE NIGHT

Looking at the neat array of swim shorts laid on his perfectly made black bed, Tom stood there wide eyed at them all. He didn't know why he was making such a big deal of it. Did it really matter what swim shorts he wore?

Wanting to take his mind of this strangely big decision, Tom raised his head. Instantly regretting doing that as he saw all the piles or collapsed piles of clothes around his large bedroom. He knew his bedroom had wonderful brown hardwood floors but... they were slightly taken over by various piles of dirty clothes.

Equally the entire bedroom was a mess. The very nice large mirror on his built in wardrobe only hide the mess within. It had taken Tom at least an hour to find these pairs of swim shorts.

But at least the entire flat didn't smell of sweat and sadly tears. Instead, Tom had make sure to buy a few scented candles so the flat smelt of cloves and spices. Making the taste of carrot cake form in Tom's mouth.

Hearing the evening traffic of London starting to build up with all the honking of cars and swearing of drivers, Tom looked out the massive clear windows of his high rise flat. The beautiful London landscape starting to change from its boring and chaotic commuter daytime to its fun and amazing nighttime. Especially on a Friday night.

As the sky started to turn a beautiful fiery orange, the Shard and other wonderful London landmarks started to light up.

But this made Tom know he needed to hurry up and go to this silly hot tub party. But he knew he didn't really want to go.

It wasn't that he didn't want to see his friends after a hard week at work but a part of Tom just wanted to relax at home. Maybe watch a film and hopefully meet someone on Grindr. Because as much as he loved his friends that was probably their only flaw. They were all straight and Tom was the only gay they knew. Making them great at being friends and people to hang out with but not the best for meeting boys with.

Well, Tom did smile a little at the horrific attempt his bestie Ruby made once to introduce him to a guy. They didn't go well. Tom even remembered getting a drink thrown in his face. Was it bad that Tom just wanted to spend the night at home hoping to find a boyfriend online?

Looking at the swim shorts laid out in front of him, Tom knew he had to go. He loved his friends and Ruby would never forgive him for not going.

Reaching down and picking up a bright blue pair of shorts, Tom felt the smooth material in between his fingers. It felt good. Tom knew it looked great on and a fair number of boys had mentioned that fact at the sauna. But he was going out with friends, straight ones at that, he couldn't dress to impress. Could he?

Shaking his head, Tom put them down and picked up a black pair. The material felt worn but smooth in his hand and a hint of lavender conditioner filled the air.

Tom remembered the last time he wore these shorts. That was a fun evening with his friends at a water park. With the whirlpool and Ruby almost getting kicked out by a very hot lifeguard.

Smiling at those memories, Tom grabbed the shorts and looked out the window to see the amazing London evening-scape. It was going to be a great night. So Tom headed out to the hot tub party. Maybe something memorable would happen again?

***

As the hot water of the large water hot tub made his body warm and his skin wonderfully relaxed, Neil definitely knew he loved the hot tub. He didn't know why he had said no to Ruby before. This was great!

Looking up at the pink tiled walls of this large hot tub room in Ruby's penthouse flat, Neil couldn't believe how she could afford it.

He had known Ruby for months now since he first moved to London and as far as he knew she didn't appear to have a high paid job. Neil thought she did something in publishing but Ruby never said what exactly.

Looking at the hot tub and the expensive brand name, Neil guessed this was certainly family money. But Ruby was a great person so he didn't care.

The smell of chlorine made Neil relax even more for some strange reason then the sound of kissing reminded Neil he wasn't alone. But he would happily be alone in this wonderfully warm hot tub.

Looking over, Neil felt uncomfortable as Ruby in her bright pink bikini that (supposedly) highlighted her slim, attractive frame and her youthful smooth features. Continued to make out with her boyfriend Kieran.

Now Neil could happily look at Kieran all night with his tight shorts, massive muscles and strong jawline. But the two of them making out in front of him just made Neil uncomfortable.

A part of Neil wondered when this new person Ruby had mentioned was meant to arrive. Neil remembered Ruby saying they would get on great but dear, sweet Ruby... wasn't to be trusted when she said that. The stories Neil needed to forget. The people Ruby thought were gay and weren't made Neil be laughed at or worse more times than he could count. But Ruby was a great friend so he laughed about it.

After this week at his job though, Neil really wouldn't mind something good happening. Even if it was just someone to talk to for the rest of the night and maybe make a new friend. The last thing Neil wanted was to be an awkward third wheel on what looked like Ruby and Kieran's first date in a while.

Looking away and focusing on the warm water gently run over his skin, Neil thought about his various attempts at dating. Up north he had had so many bad relationships, Neil didn't want to think about them anymore.

Then he bit his lip as he thought about his last boyfriend and how badly that had ended. The heartache, the trouble at work and the uncomfortable home life. Neil wasn't going to let that happen again.

In all honesty, Neil hoped moving to London might be easier. There was plenty of insurance work after all but the boys here seemed so clicky and only interested in hook ups. He didn't want that. He just wanted... something real. Something he hadn't had for a long time.

A loud bird sound echoed around the flat multiple times as someone ran the doorknob.

Neil had to smile as Ruby hopped out the hot tub and walked to the door. Leaving a long trail of water behind her.

He had no idea what to expect. Neil hadn't met too many of Ruby's friends. What if he didn't like him? Or worse, what if this friend didn't like him?

Neil liked hanging out with Ruby. He didn't want to be kicked out because this friend didn't like him.

Knowing he was being ridiculous, Neil took a long deep breath, tasting the horrid chlorine in his mouth and focused on just acting normal. He didn't need to be nervous. This was just a friend of Ruby's.

Hearing two sets of footsteps coming back, Neil tried to act cool as Ruby stepped into the hot tub. She looked at Neil and smiled. Then Neil turned back to look at the door.

Wow!

Neil couldn't help but smile at this honestly stunning guy that walked in and stared at Neil. He was beautiful. This Mystery Guy was stunning with his handsome youthful face and his strong jawline. His wonderful hazelnut hair was parted perfectly to the left and his tight little black shorts were... great.

Neil tried to force himself to look at something else but he couldn't. Mystery Guy was perfection.

Even better he kept smiling at Neil.

***

Seeing Ruby walk ahead into the hot tub room, Tom stopped for a moment to think. As if looking at the posh paintings hanging on the corridor walls would buy him time, Tom looked at them and thought. He could smell the strong chlorine and the hot steam covered his skin even from out here. His stomach twisted.

Tom didn't know whether or not he should go in. He didn't know this new person and what if they were horrible. Ruby had a cute habit of picking hot guys that turned out to be jerks. Could Tom really handle going through more rejection?

He just wanted something real and fun. Was that really much to ask?

Deciding he had to go in, Tom walked forward into the hot tub. He really didn't want to look at the people at first so he looked at the interesting (?) choice of pink tiles that lined the hot tub room. It was hot in here. Sweat had already started to pour off him.

Turning his attention to the hot tub, Tom made sure not to smile at Kieran (despite him looking great) and he gave Ruby an awkward little nod to her then… oh!

Tom couldn't help himself but smile at this New Guy. He was hot lying there in the hot tub!

His chiselled, defined jaw and amazing face. He looked like some kind of model. Trust Ruby to know models!

The water covered and made New Guy's skin (and amazing muscles) shine. He was… beautiful.

Ruby cut through the silence. "Tom fab you make it. This is Neil,"

Tom couldn't stop smiling. Neil was a posh, hot name.

Ruby turned to Neil. "Neil, this is Tom,"

It didn't look like Neil could speak so he gave Tom a massive smile and nod.

Without hesitating (anymore), Tom stepped into the hot tub. Feeling the warm water cover his skin up to his chest. He turned to look at Neil.

"I knew you two would get along fab," Ruby said.

"It's nice to meet you, Tom," Neil said, giving Tom a boyish smile.

"Same. Has Ruby gotten you into trouble yet?" Tom asked.

Neil looked at Ruby. "If you mean getting drinks throw at me and shouted at. Yes,"

Tom bit his lip and smiled. This was going to be a great night. Finally, another person to complain or mock Ruby with!

"Rub told Neil about the lifeguard?"

Ruby buried her face in Kieran's shoulders. Tom paused for a brief moment, before tonight he would have been jealous. Now he couldn't care less. Odd?

"Neil, me and some friends went to a water park. Rub sees a hot lifeguard. Grabs me. Tries to pimp me to him and- well- he wasn't happy,"

"That was a fab day and you know it! And that Lifeguard was hot and he was checking out Tom,"

"He was checking me out because you were next to me!"

Ruby cocked her head. "Oh,"

As much as Tom loved Ruby, she was utterly hopeless for romance at times. A part of Tom was amazed she had been with Kieran for so long.

Kieran moved about in the water for a moment, but Tom kept looking at Neil.

"Where do you come from Neil? You sound Northern," Kieran asked.

"You speak southern," Tom said.

Neil smiled. "I was raised in the North but my parents made sure I spoke *proper*,"

Kieran shook his head. Clearly expecting a more interesting story.

"Oh Ruby was telling me you were thinking about leaving London," Kieran asked.

Neil gave Tom a quick look. "That was just a thought. I may or may not. Depends if something keeps me here,"

After another half an hour of talking, Tom had to admit this was great. He hadn't talked this freely for months maybe years. Talking with Neil was so easy. They spoke about their love of books, London and their various relationships. This was great, but was it too great?

And that was before Tom thought about Neil leaving London. It was stupid but Tom didn't want that to happen. They had only just met but that didn't mean it didn't bother Tom.

The sound of Ruby standing up and the warm water rushing off her made Tom turn his focus to her. She came over and tapped him on the shoulder.

"Tom, come with me. I need helping with the drinks,"

Standing up, Tom didn't really want to leave. He wanted to stay and talk to Neil. He didn't know what he wanted to talk about, Tom just wanted to. But he didn't want his interest to be too intense so he stood up and looked at Neil before walking out with Ruby.

***

Watching Tom walk away with his beautiful body moving smoothly and perfectly, Neil felt his spirit fall a little. He didn't want to see Tom go. Hell, this was the first time since coming to London, he had felt comfortable.

All the hurrying and chaos of London was too much sometimes, that was part of the reason Neil wanted to leave London. But maybe if London was filled with people like Tom then maybe it wasn't so bad.

Maybe Neil just needed to stay a bit longer and get to know this hot guy.

The feeling of moving warm water made Neil feel relaxed but this didn't distract him from his problems.

Of course, he wanted to spend time with Tom and see him. Maybe learn a bit more but he had done this so many times before. Every single time was meant to be different and with new (or old) faces. And every time Neil got involved and opened up to these people, he got hurt.

The last breakup was too bad. Neil couldn't go through that again. It didn't matter that it happened between him and a work friend. It still happened and hurt so much.

Staring at the rather nice pink tiles that lined the room, Neil thought about the typical London boys he had met. They were interested in hook ups only. Sure they were fun but Neil just wanted something real.

Would Tom be interested in that?

"What you thinking about?" Kieran asked.

Despite him not knowing much about Kieran, Neil did want to know a bit more about Tom.

"What sort of boys does Tom like?"

Kieran laughed and looked at the ceiling.

Neil didn't know what was funny.

"Ruby knew this would happen. You like him?"

Neil didn't want to seem easy or predictable but he shook his head anyway.

"Just ask him out. Tom's a great guy. Kind, easy to talk to. Just take a chance,"

"Did Ruby tell you to say that?"

Kieran nodded. "She just wants to be a matchmaker. You know she tries to make people happy,"

Kieran did have a point, but Ruby had made so many mistakes. Neil always made sure he laughed them off to her but they hurt. They really hurt. A guy can only take so many drinks in the face, awkward moments and rejection.

What if Tom was just another bad choice from Ruby?

"Ask him out," Kieran said as he got out of the hot tub and wiped himself with a towel. "Great seeing you again. I need to get up early tomorrow,"

"Bye," Neil said, as Kieran walked away.

A part of Neil was happy that Kieran was gone. For some reason he liked the idea of there being one less person in the hot tub. One less person between him and Tom. Maybe he would ask Tom out.

***

Feeling the cold black plastic seat of the high stool under him, Tom sat at the high marble table of Ruby's Kitchen. Tracing the black veins of the smooth marble with his fingers as he thought about life and most importantly Neil.

The smell of strong vodka, pineapple and other

sweet exotic fruits made Tom smile, as the taste of sweet fruity sugar formed on his tongue. And a memory of his 18th birthday party came into his mind. Ruby was a good friend that night. She was always a good friend.

Raising his head slightly, Tom admired the amazing kitchen Ruby had in her penthouse apartment. The kitchen was probably bigger than Tom's entire flat. High end, expensive gadgets and tools lined all the walls. Hiding under the worktops.

A part of Tom was tempted to be cruel by asking Ruby what each one was and how it worked. But he knew she had no idea. That's why she had Kieran. Her strong, perfect man that did things for her.

Looking at Ruby in front of him, Tom admired how quickly and artfully she mixed the drinks. Including a rather strange looking long glass filled with pink juice and slices of pineapple.

She always had his best interests at heart. Tom knew Ruby was a type of friend that acted like the care-free, wildcard of a group. And Tom knew for a fact she WAS a wildcard. But Ruby was also the type of friend who always acted in the interest of others.

Ruby cared about Tom. She would never want to see him hurt. That still didn't make Tom feel any less uneasy.

Of course he wanted to be with Neil and explore what could happen. He was beautiful, stunning and Neil was a great guy. But Tom had thought that before about other guys and that never, ever ended well. What if he got hurt again? What if he never recovered? What if…

So many questions churned and spun round in his mind.

"You thinking about Neil? Isn't he fab?" Ruby said.

Tom looked up and smiled at her.

"Just ask him out. He must care about you. I know him. He is absolutely fab. Perfect even,"

"You've said that before," Tom said.

"Yes but Neil is different. He is just so kind and perfect. What's holding you back?"

"What if he doesn't like me?"

"Oh Tommy, he keeps looking at you. He keeps checking you out. He loves you. He's-"

"Please don't say fab,"

"He's fabulous," Ruby said.

Tom smiled and shook his head.

Ruby walked over to Tom and hugged him.

"Tommy, we're known each other for ten years. God, I need to get a life,"

Tom playfully jabbed her in the ribs.

"Tommy though, I have never hurt you or tried to. Have I?"

Tom shook his head.

Ruby was about to say something when Kieran walked in and kissed Ruby before whispering something in her ear. She smiled. Kieran walked off presumably to bed.

Normally, Tom would watch Kieran walk away but this time he really didn't want to. He knew that had to be a sign but… actually it was a sign.

Tom smiled as he realised since meeting Neil he hadn't thought or even looked at another guy (even Kieran who was usually very hot).

Looking around, Tom saw that he was alone. He shook his head when he realised Kieran was probably inviting Ruby to bed.

The sound of wet footsteps came from behind and Tom felt a warm badly dried arm wrap around him. His skin buzzed and it was like a spark rushed through him.

Looking up, Tom couldn't happy but smile as he looked into Neil's strong beautiful eyes and felt his great stunning body pressed against him.

This really was the time to stop being afraid. Ruby always wanted the best for him, so Tom was going to take a chance, trust his friend and enjoy this moment and hopefully many more.

"I think I might stay in London if you want that," Neil said.

Tom's smile deepened. This was going to be fun. A chance to spend more time and hopefully do a lot more together.

So as Tom stood up, gently held Neil's soft warm hand in his own. Tom led him back to the hot tub as his stomach and head went light. This was going to be a memorable night and hopefully many more memorable nights to come.

LOVE IN HALLS

As he closed the cold wooden door and heard the lock click, Zach smiled a little looking at his small university apartment. Well, he said apartment but it was really just a room. A small long room with a high single bed without any sheets and a wonderful long wooden desk made from Beech wood. It was a wonderful colour.

Then Zach's eye went to the poorly yellow carpeted floor with all his stuff in boxes lying there just waiting there to be packed away. From his bedding to his cooking stuff to his textbooks and all the other university things your course tells you to have.

Admiring the plain white walls of his apartment, Zach felt the cold air flow past him as he realised his mother must have opened a window before she and Zach's father had left him. But the smell of harsh cleaning chemicals still filled the air.

As much as Zach loved the idea of coming to the University of Kent in the south of England, he was nervous. He only lived half an hour away by car but he still felt nervous. This was so new to him. Whilst he had been away from home before weeks at a time, they were always times with his friends and people who knew. He was here alone at university.

Of course, Zach knew university was meant to be a time of adventure, new discovery and fun but he hated parties. He never liked them so the idea of university had scared him at first. With Zach wanting to commune to and from university so he could still be with his friends and parents.

It was only when his best friend and the only person who knew he was gay mentioned that going and living at university would give Zach a chance to meet other gay people. Then he got more interested about living at university.

And in all honesty the university campus in historical Canterbury was beautiful, the buildings were clean, great and very fit for purpose. Especially, the law building that was great, except for the weird way the rooms were laid out. Zach knew it was going to be trying to navigate those corridors!

But now Zach was here at university, he wasn't sure if his plan to meet other gay people would work. He had tried to find out how to meet them online and Zach still didn't understand fully. There was an LGBT+ society (which was like a social group) but he was still nervous.

He was nervous about so many things but the feelings of loneliness didn't help. For the first time in his life, Zach felt completely alone at university and judging by the events on this week, so freshers could meet each other and socialise. Zach wasn't convinced his feelings of loneliness were going to ease.

In an ideal world that would be an opportunity for people who didn't like drinking and partying to hang out. A part of Zach was sure those places did exist but he didn't know how to find them!

And the massive thing that concerned Zach was what if his parents found out he was gay. They would absolutely hate him but Zach had tried to be the good straight boy for so long and his mental health had gone so many times. Was it so wrong Zach wanted to have fun and love whoever he wanted?

Zach wanted university to give him an opportunity to find out more about himself so bad. He just wanted to experience love and fun for once in his university life before he returned to his straight conservative family.

The sound of people running up and down the corridor outside but Zach smile for a brief moment. He knew he wasn't really alone and there were 7 other rooms in this area or the section of the corridor that he shared a kitchen with. He could easily find friends.

Looking back at his boxes of stuff and Zach opened one of the cardboard boxes. The cardboard feeling cold and smooth in between his fingers. When he saw the box was full of his cooking equipment, Zach took a deep breath and decided to go to the kitchen. He had to met new people and a part of him really hoped there was a hot (hopefully gay) guy here.

***

Looking at the small black chipboard table in the middle of the shared kitchen, Max had to smile at it. He had seen some awful university accommodations on the different opening days at different universities. But some of the worse places still had a good looking table.

But aside from that Max loved this kitchen, a row of reasonably large individual white cupboards went around the top of the kitchen at head height and another row was underneath the black chipboard worktops.

Smelling the horrid chemical filled air that left a pleasant lemony taste in his mouth, Max walked over to one of the large clear windows that went the entire length of the far wall. But you could only open the top windows.

Max thought that was sensible the last thing you wanted when they're having a party in the kitchen is have someone fall out the window. They were on the ground floor but still!

Max couldn't believe how excited he was about going to university. He was actually here after years of hard work, he was here at university studying economics.

He couldn't wait to go out and explore Canterbury from the historical cathedral to the museums to the student life. It was going to be great.

And Max had heard there was a great gay scene at all universities so he really wanted to go to that. A great chance to meet people and get to know other gays. (and maybe meet a boy for fun)

The closest Max had come to meeting other gay people were his school friends but Max just wanted to meet more. Because the problem with gay schoolfriends in the rural north of England is you can't experience wider gay culture. Which was another reason Max wanted, needed to come to a university near London.

Looking at his black plastic box of kitchen pots, pans and utensils on the wooden kitchen floor, Max didn't know where to begin. He had already filled his shelf in the fridge with his food and filled one of his cupboards with dry food.

Opening his white cupboard below the worktop, Max was surprised at the amount of space in it. He could definitely fit all his pots and pans in here and the utensils.

Pulling his plastic box over, the plastic feeling rough in his hand, Max started to put all the different things into the cupboard.

With his head buried in the cupboard trying to make a very annoying pot fit inside another one, Max heard the kitchen door buzz open, shut and another person walked in before stopping at the other end of the kitchen.

Max knew the polite thing to do was to stop and say hello to this new person straight away. But he wanted to make sure this pot fitted in the cupboard.

After a few moments it did and Max looked up and oh... Max was in trouble.

As he stared at this utterly beautiful boy with his back to Max wearing a pair of tight black jeans, a loose top that still highlighted how fit this boy was and his short blondish brown hair looked amazing.

A part of Max really wanted the Mystery Boy or man. It was the more appropriate term because they were all over 18 here. Max really wanted Mystery Man to turn around, he wanted to look at this man's face. It had to be beautiful.

Then Max started to notice the horrible chemical smell to the air had gone to be replaced with Mystery Man's strong beautiful earthy aftershave. He smelt great.

As his hands started to go a little sweaty and his head started to go light, the logical part of Max wanted to slap himself. He never acted like this not even around his insanely hot friend Callum at school. Max was a calculated, cool, outgoing student, not a constantly horny teenager.

But as Max admired this beautiful Mystery, he didn't care for what he was meant to be like. Mystery man was beautiful and if Max got the chance to spend the next year living near him then that was great.

Max's smile grew as Mystery man returned around to face him and Max got to look at his beautiful face. Those deep stunning rich blue eyes and his smooth perfect face all topped off by a boyish grin that made Max's stomach twist and turn inside.

After a few moments of looking at this beautiful Mystery Man, it dawned on Max. Mystery Man was staring at him and smiling. This could be great but he needed to make sure he didn't make it awkward first.

***

Pressing his small white key card against the large wooden kitchen door, it buzzed as it opened and Zach walked in. It was a bit of a challenge walking in holding a large cold cardboard box filled with kitchen equipment but Zach managed.

He couldn't believe that even the kitchen still stunk of the same harsh chemicals that his bedroom smelt of. But at least the kitchen left a strangely pleasant lemony taste in his mouth.

At first glance, Zach wasn't sure what he thought of the small shared kitchen. The wooden floor and black chipboard dining table in the centre of the room and the worktops were somewhat unexpected. Zach would have thought the chipboard would be covered up. Even if it was just covered with some plastic of some sort it would have looked better.

At least the shared kitchen had a great amount of

cupboard space as Zach walked up to his dedicated cupboards. Two large white cupboards, one at head height and the other below the worktop.

Looking at the other end of the kitchen, Zach smiled as there was another guy kneeling down to get into his cupboard.

Turning away so Zach could start to fill his cupboard with his own pots and pans, Zach started to feel excited for some reason. He supposed it could have been because the idea of going to university was finally hitting him. Zach could actually meet new people and socialise with new different types of people that his conservative family never would have let him socialise with.

That thought alone was enough to make Zach excited. He wondered what this new person was like and what he studied. As much as Zach appreciated most degrees he really hoped this man didn't do a boring degree.

But thinking that Zach smiled, a lot of people would have called his degree boring. Who wants to know about law? It's boring and Zach agreed to some extent. There were some boring parts of the law but it was amazing to be aware of the laws so you could use them.

Placing the last pot in his cupboard at head height, Zach felt like he was being watched so he made sure the final pot was safe inside (the last thing he needed was a pot jumping out at him) and he turned around.

Wow!

Zach instantly didn't know what to do as his stomach did flips and the butterflies inside him broke free. He didn't know what was happening.

Looking at this stunning, perfect guy in front of him, Zach didn't know what to look at first. He was so beautiful. The Flatmate had perfect light green eyes like emeralds that seemed to sparkle in the light and his slim frame was clearly a lie for a slightly muscular body beneath with a six pack. After years of PE classes, Zach knew the type of bodies that appeared not to be muscled but they were. The Flatmate was stunning.

It was all topped off by the smooth perfect blond hair parted precisely to the left, like all the Flatmate had done was swirl his head and it was perfect. He was so beautiful. And that movie star smile.

As Zach started to feel his heart speed up, he didn't know what was going on. He had never felt like this before but he had never seen a man as beautiful as Flatmate before. Was this normal?

Zach took a deep breath as he tried to understand what was happening to him. Was he attracted to Flatmate?

A part of him blamed his parents entirely for feeling like this, if they had allowed him to be who he was then he wouldn't be panicking about feeling like this now.

Then he realised Flatmate was also smiling back at him. Was he interested? Was he pleased? Was this a straight person thing to smile at another man?

Flatmate started to walk over to Zach, and he could smell Flatmate's sweet manly scent.

"Hi I'm Max," Flatmate said.

Max.

Zach smiled at the name alone. That was a great sweet name, a manly, perfect name.

Again Zach didn't know why he was making

such a big deal out of learning a name. But looking at Max, he really didn't care.

"Hey, I'm Zach,"

Max smiled and Zach felt a little flattered. No one had ever smiled at him like that before.

"What you studying?" Zach asked. It was a basic line, but it always worked at university.

"Economics. You?" Max said.

Whilst Zach had no idea what economics covered except the economy, he wanted to play it cool.

"Interesting. I'm doing Law,"

Max smiled at Zach. "You don't know a thing about economics do you?"

Zach looked to the floor for a moment. "Is it that obvious?"

Max placed his hand on the worktop and caught Zach's finger. Zach didn't want his finger to move as blood rushed to his head (and other places). It felt amazing. Then Zach realised he was so out of touch with himself. Was it normal to be so excited by a touch?

"Oh sorry," Max said, moving his hand away.

Zach frowned for a brief second.

"When did you get here?" Max asked.

"This morning. My parents had work so they didn't wanna make a day of it,"

"I'm sorry," Max said, clearly hearing the sadness in Zach's voice.

Zach felt strange another man saying that to him. The closest he got to another man saying something kind or gentle to him was years ago before secondary (high) school.

"It's okay. I'm sure they have some conservative

church stuff to do later anyway,"

Max leant forward, he was so close Zach would feel his body warmth and Zach savoured this sweet manly scent. Of course he wanted to kick himself for acting so weirdly or *gay* but he didn't care. A small part of him wanted his parents to see him like this. Not only because he was happy but because they would be so disappointed.

"They don't like gays," Max said with a boyish grin.

Zach smiled with a grin of his own. "Not one bit, why I wanna come to university. Get to meet some people,"

Max nodded and leant back. Zach's spirit fell a little as Zach moved away.

"I'm going to an LGBT+ event tonight. Not a party. Just a meet and greet. You should come. I'll be there. It be *nice* to see you," Max said, passing Zach a leaflet of where the event was.

Zach got the leaflet and stared for an extra few seconds into Max's beautiful green emerald eyes.

"See you tonight maybe," Max said as he picked up his black plastic box and left.

Zach looked at the little leaflet with where the meet and greet was, he wasn't sure whether to go or not.

***

Feeling the cold September evening air blow past him gently, Max stood outside a large white rectangular building with a rather nice looking grassy bit outside with a few blue flowers.

Max leant against the rough white brick wall as he pressed his back into it, he really wanted Zach to turn up. He wanted to see him and get talking to him some more.

They both felt their excitement and happiness when Max had honestly accidentally touched Zach earlier. But he was very glad he did it, maybe it was his mind trying to see if Zach was remotely interested. If that's what his mind was doing then Max needed to give himself more credit than normal. It had worked but Max just wanted to see Zach.

He wanted to look into those beautiful deep rich blue eyes and admire that stunning face. Even the thought of Zach made Max smile and his head went light quickly.

Breathing in the cold evening air that smelt refreshing and crisp, Max was a bit nervous. He had put his heart on the line for a beautiful but unsure man. What if Zach wasn't gay after all? What if he only thought he was but when it came down to it he was straight going through a phase?

Or even worse what if his parents found out and got angry at Zach? That was Max's true concern, it wasn't about himself but Zach. He was extremely grateful his parents loved him and accepted his *weirdness* as they joked. But Max was hardly blind to the fact other people weren't so lucky.

What if Zach got hurt too? Max frowned a little as he wondered if this was Zach's first relationship or love interest. It probably was, making Max a little unsure about if he should get with Zach if the opportunity came up. He wasn't sure if he was first material.

Sure a lot of boys had said Max was great and they loved him, but they still left him. They still abandoned him.

Looking out over the amazing university campus

with its wide open grass fields and wonderful white buildings with lots of other university students walking about with friends. The sound of laughter and chatting filled the air. Max smiled at their happiness and how these people were all coping with the move to university.

He honestly didn't know how Zach was going to cope especially with how Zach had sounded earlier. That beautiful man even looked a bit shy and nervous about meeting his flatmates for the next year. What if a meet and greet was too much?

A final burst of laughter from friends walking back or to god knows where made Max realise that he didn't care about his own feelings. He was definitely going to wait and see if Zach was coming. Max wanted Zach more than anything and he wasn't going anywhere. He was going to wait for him.

***

Walking towards the building with the meet and greet, Zach couldn't stop smiling as he slowly made his way there.

Feeling the cold, refreshing and crisp smelling air blow gently past him, Zach knew this was going to be the start of a great first year at university.

Looking ahead at the mini black tarmac road ahead of him, Zach knew it wouldn't be a long walk to the building and hopefully Max.

A part of him couldn't handle the thought of Max not being there. Zach wanted to see Max more than anything.

He almost laughed at himself as Zach remembered the panic and hurry he was in putting away all of his cupboard boxes trying to find clothes for tonight. Thankfully, Zach had managed to find a great freshly pressed white shirt that showed off his slim body and a pair of tight dark, dark blue jeans.

Judging by the reactions Zach had gotten from girls as he walked it seemed to be flattering. Zach hoped Max would find it attractive.

Continuing to walk towards the meet and greet, Zach started to walk a bend in the tarmac road as the road continued towards the group of buildings at the centre of the university campus.

A part of him was still shouting at Zach not to do this but that was the years or maybe even decade of forcing himself to be a good straight boy for his parents. But Zach just wanted a little taste of freedom tonight and maybe the rest of the university year.

What Zach really wanted was just to know what being gay was like. He wanted to experience what talking about boys was like and what one felt like.

Of course, Zach knew these thoughts sounded silly to other gay people, so he definitely wasn't going to tell Max. But to him these were so important, like a dirty little secret.

Zach started to turn onto the main university campus and in the far distance he could make out the amazing body shape of Max, and Zach stopped.

His stomach churned and the butterflies within him went crazy. Zach so badly wanted this but he hesitated.

What if his parents found out? What if he went to this meet and greet tonight and Max became his boyfriend? (Even the thought of that made him the most excited he'd ever been)

It surely wasn't right on Max to date him for a year, dump him when Zach went back home and blank him during Christmas and other times he went back home. That wasn't fair.

Hearing the other freshers laughing, chatting and being happy, Zach had to smile. All these amazing other people were happy and having a good time, so why couldn't he?

There was absolutely nothing stopping him and a year of being himself and truly being happy meant everything to him. And maybe it could give him the confidence to stand up to his parents if they ever found out.

Zach walked on.

After a few moments, Zach's mouth dropped at how beautiful and utterly gorgeous Max looked in his own very tight white shirt that showed off his amazing body and his six pack. (Zach knew he was muscular!) And Max's tight black jeans looked great too.

As soon as Max saw Zach he looked into Zach's beautiful eyes, Zach didn't care about what anyone except Max thought. So he gave him a massive hug. Pure magic and electricity filled them both as they hugged.

Zach breathed in Max's wonderful earthy, manly aftershave and held his hand.

Turning around and walking into the meet and greet, Zach knew for a fact this was going to be a great first year at university and hopefully a lot, lot longer.

THE ONE THAT GOT AWAY

Looking around his little London apartment, Brad looked at the smooth cold brown oak floor for his keys. He could have sworn he had seen them a moment ago. Those things were nightmares.

In case he had missed them, Brad looked at the brown wooden table and chest of drawers that lined the smooth white walls of his apartment. The keys weren't there but Brad could still see so much junk like letters and opened cardboard boxes that needed to be sorted. Including a ton of boxes next to him.

Brad knew he had only arrived yesterday in London and he had spent all morning and early afternoon unpacking, but he wanted to have unpacked all his things by now. At least he had the rest of the afternoon and evening to sort out his clothes and other things from the boxes.

But he needed to find his keys first because Brad did need to get some milk. The cute little sachets of milk his mother had probably stolen for him had all run out sadly. Getting milk sounds easy, except he had no idea where the nearest corner shop was. Did they even have corner shops here in London or was everything a supermarket?

Those simple questions made Brad smile a little as he got excited for the day ahead. He just had a feeling that this was going to be a great first day in London.

Breathing in the sweet, cedarwood air from an air freshener he had going, Brad checked his pockets and surprisingly enough (not) they weren't there. Where were they?

Casting his mind back to Dover in the far south of England, Brad felt a wave of emotion wash over him as he remembered the great friends and boyfriend he had left behind.

But in all fairness the beautiful boyfriend had made it clear to him, Brad wasn't worth his time and going to London for a new job was pointless. Also there was some moaning about Brad not being able to commit to him, but Brad didn't believe him. After all, it was always Brad who had done everything in their relationship. Maybe, no, Brad was definitely better off without him.

Walking away from the conversation and that amazing relationship was next to impossible for Brad, but he did it. He actually did it.

A part of Brad was naturally proud of himself for doing it and forging his own path in life. Yet that didn't mean it didn't hurt.

Then another part of Brad still felt like this was a terrible idea. Moving so far away from the people who loved him and the job that was secure and had some great managers. Compared to so-called cutthroat London.

Brad forced those thoughts away as he walked forward and felt something cold and metallic press into his foot. Looking down Brad shook his head as he saw it was his keys. Picking them up Brad carefully placed them in his pocket.

Looking at a cardboard box next to him, Brad brushed his fingers over the smooth cardboard and saw the edge of a brilliant card his best friend Victoria had written him before Brad left. She asked him a simple question in the card because she had to go aboard sadly before he left. Victoria asked him *why he had to go?*

Brad knew there was nothing hurtful or sad about the card, his best friend wanted the best for him and Victoria had promised to visit him as soon as she returned.

Yet it still made Brad think because, of course, he was young so he wanted to explore and live his own life beyond Dover. But he really wanted to experience the gay nightlife here in London. Sure, the southeast and south had some great gay clubs but there was just something about London that was alluring. After all, London was the gay capital of the UK, and maybe Europe but Brad wasn't sure.

Sadly Brad couldn't say that to Victoria,

especially with how close her and his parents were. Just the thought of the conversations that would spark between Brad's parents made him smile and almost laugh.

Turning around and placing his fingers on the warm metal doorknob, Brad turned it slowly as he knew for some strange reason this was going to be a wonderful day. The end of his first day in London was going to be rememberable.

***

Stepping outside of his high rise London workplace, Harry walked to one side and pressed his slim, suited back against the warm metal of the building.

He knew it must have looked weird and lots of his colleagues basically ran from the office after work. But Harry always liked to rest for a few minutes before going home. Harry liked to think of it as moving his mindset from the uptight business accountant to the more relaxed and fun person he was.

Looking around and breathing in the strange smelling mixture of car exhaust and fresh air, Harry looked at all the blocks of grey high rise London skyscrapers around him.

That was one of his favourite things about London. It was such a weird combination of the old buildings with their stunning architecture with the new modern buildings. In a lot of places, it looked great. In other parts of London not so much sadly.

Then turning his attention to street level, Harry smiled to himself as he saw the normal flood of commuters and other office workers as it was rush hour.

Definitely something he was surprised at when he first moved to London, over six months ago, Harry wasn't expecting the commuter rush hour to be this bad.

Even the tube and London taxis for chaotic and packed full with all the different officer workers.

Harry gave a little smile to himself as he felt a little smug over all the other office workers, because when his accounting firm had headhunted him from a rival after university. They sold him an apartment nearby. It was wonderful. And it meant Harry could and happily would avoid the overcrowded and very sweaty tube.

Granted Harry wouldn't mind getting sweaty with some of the other hot workers on the tube. Those men were hot!

Pushing the thought away from him, Harry heard other commuters chatting and laughing and he decided he probably should make a move. He needed to get home and prepare for some silly work function tonight. So much as moving to his fun relaxed mindset for too long.

Stepping forward, Harry stretched for a moment and started to walk into the crowd.

He crashed into someone.

His head hit another.

Someone grabbed him.

Harry grabbed too.

Looking up, Harry's eyes widened and he instantly smiled as he looked into the beautiful deep brown eyes of a Gorgeous Man. Harry couldn't believe how amazing this man looked with his square handsome face, short brown hair that blew angelically in the gentle wind and his killer smile that melted Harry's heart.

Feeling that other people were trying to get past them, Gorgeous Man moved him and Harry other to one side, next to Harry's workplace.

A little voice in Harry's mind was telling him to recognise who it was. It felt as if Harry knew Gorgeous Man but he couldn't place it.

Noticing Gorgeous Man was still holding Harry gently with his soft smooth hands holding Harry's arms. He started to remember something. It was at a time back at school over ten years ago on the last day of school at some party in the evening.

Harry remembered a hot guy holding him just like this and they kissed in secret. Harry's friends couldn't know he was gay. Hell, they still didn't know.

As Harry looked deeper into those beautiful dark brown eyes, it twigged who Gorgeous Man was. It was his old best friend Brad, the one who got away and Harry's biggest regret so far.

***

Walking along the busy London street with tall high rise skyscrapers rising high into the sky with their cold dark grey metal cladding, and massive glass windows either side of him. Brad thought this was amazing.

As he felt the rough, hard pathway under his feet, Brad couldn't help but admire these massive, tall buildings as everyone left them. Presumably for the London rush hour, but Brad hadn't expected rush hour to be this busy.

There were hundreds of people on the pathway with lots and lots of black London cabs stopping and picking up passengers.

All these people were in various types of office wear. From tall and short young and old women in dresses and posh suits. To the very hot young new office workers hurrying to get to the tube before rush hour really set in.

Brad smelt in all their different scents and aftershaves and perfumes. From the great flowery and sweet perfume of the ladies to the amazing smelly manly aftershaves. This was quite a nice trip for a new boy in London.

Hearing the honking cab horns and people talking amongst themselves and into large expensive phones, Brad reminded himself that he was starting work on Monday, and if a Friday rush hour was this bad, he hated to think what a Monday one would be like.

Continuing to walk (and dodge people) through the busy London pathway, Brad tried to think about what to do tonight. Of course he needed to unpack the rest of his things but he had all weekend to do that. Maybe he could go to Soho, the real gay capital.

Brad quickly dismissed the thought as he realised if he bought a boy back, they would probably leave at the sight of his apartment. Maybe he wouldn't be doing that. But-

Brad walked into someone.

The person moaned.

Brad grabbed them.

He looked at the person.

The other person looked back and oh... Brad couldn't believe who it was. He would recognise that beautiful youthful face anywhere with that smooth stunning smile, and looked so boyish and suggestive. Even this sexy guy's hair was just as he remembered it. Perfectly blond and wonderfully short on the sides but long on top.

And in that beautiful tight suit that highlighted everything wonderful about this guy. Brad smiled as he saw his old (but utterly stunning) best friend Harry.

Harry was still just as beautiful as the day he had broken Brad's heart. Brad never wanted that night to happen but at school he was openly gay and he loved it. He was part of the sporty crowd as was Harry and they were fine with him being gay. (A surprising fact at the time) So at that last night celebrating the end of school, Harry had kissed him so much.

Brad frowned as he remembered the rest of the night when Harry had come back to his place.

Nothing happened sadly. But he left early next morning without saying a word.

That had hurt Brad so much. Harry had even blocked him on all the social media sites and by text and phone. An amazing kiss but Harry got away.

Realising he was holding Harry's wonderful forearms and he was actually sweating slightly, Brad thought what would he do now. This was clearly weird. After ten years suddenly running into the beautiful schoolboy crush.

He heard someone and lots of other people trying to get past so Brad gently moved Harry to one side. Next to another high rise London skyscraper.

In that moment, Brad thought about how great Harry felt. It was like pure chemistry was going through them as Brad looked at Harry's amazing face, he was so beautiful.

Then he realised he needed to do something, this was clearly weird and he hated himself for being so weird. He was always the cool, straight acting gay kid at school. He certainly wasn't like that now.

"Hey Harry," Brad said, instantly regretting how lame that sounded.

Harry smiled a little more before frowning slightly.

"Hi Brad, I'm…"

Brad let go of him. "It's okay. It was over ten years ago. It's fine. I'm-"

"It's not okay. I should have stayed and explained and…"

As much as Brad loved to see Harry and he was well. This felt so weird. He loved Harry. He had always loved Harry but... Brad didn't know. All he knew was his stomach was churning and his eyes were as wide as they could be. In case this was the last time he ever saw Harry, he wanted to remember this beautiful man.

"I left you that night because I was so scared. You remember what the other guys were like. You were the only gay they liked,"

Brad had to nod at that comment. The other sporty guys still said plenty of anti-gay stuff in front of them. that was probably why he didn't contact any of them. Brad didn't know where any of them were now.

"How's your girlfriend or wife now?" Brad asked, knowing Harry had a girlfriend in school. He thought Tina was her name.

Harry gave Brad a boyish grin. "She left me shortly after school. I haven't had a girlfriend since,"

Harry kept giving Brad that beautiful boyish grin and it took Brad a few seconds to know what he meant.

Brad really smiled at that. So after all his time, Harry was actually gay. It was only then that Brad realised he had convinced himself Harry left him that night because he wasn't gay. And Brad was some drunk mistake.

The sound of people crashing into each other as they hurried to the tube reminded Brad he should probably go to. But he didn't want to. He needed to find out more about Harry and what he had been doing for the past ten years. And of course if he had a boyfriend?

Harry looked around and passed a business card to Brad. "I need to go. I got a work thing,"

Then Harry paused and Brad looked up. Admiring that beautiful, stunning face and that really suggestive smile.

"Please come tonight I want to see you. Address is on there,"

Harry gently stroked Brad's face and disappeared into the crowd.

Brad looked at the little business card and knew or hoped this was his shot.

***

Laying on his soft velvety bedsheets after having a warm, refreshing shower, Harry just stared at the posh white ceiling of his expensive penthouse apartment.

Harry had always loved this place with its massive glass walls outside the bedroom. Allowing him to admire all of London in its breath-taking beauty. He could see all the amazing sights like Westminster, the London Eye and more.

But perhaps his favourite part was all the expensive and posh appliances and glass tables in the kitchen and living area. It made him feel accomplished and posh. Something a boy from Dover rarely felt.

As Harry felt the warm, soft sheets mould to his body and breathed in his sweet orange shampoo, he remembered how hard he had worked to get here but seeing wonderful, gorgeous Brad today made it all feel slightly pointless.

Sure Harry had everything. An amazing job, a great apartment and a paycheck but he was still alone. As gorgeous Brad mentioned earlier, Harry did have a girlfriend back in the day but he was glad she left him. He never really liked her but like everything back then, he had to do these things a certain way. Otherwise he would be the freak.

Harry frowned a little at the memories of his old friends bullying Brad behind his back. Saying all sorts of horrible things about Brad just because he was different. Even Harry had said some things he hated himself for now.

Pushing himself into his bedsheet a little more, Harry thought about how much he admired Brad back at school. He was the cool, popular, confident gay kid that no one publicly picked on.

Harry always wanted to be that kid yet he never had the confidence. So when the chance came on that last night, Harry didn't hesitate he just wanted to admire and experience things with gorgeous Brad.

Harry's stomach churned a little as Harry remembered how bad he had felt after leaving Brad's house. In all honesty, Harry wasn't sure what he felt worse about. The leaving or the ghosting.

Every day he hated himself for that. It was the

least gorgeous Brad deserved after giving Harry the confidence to accept himself as gay. But Harry was afraid. He was always afraid of people thinking of him as weird, deluded or all those other silly terms used to describe his kind. And they were his kind.

Turning his head to look at the massive mirrored built-in wardrobe next to his bed, Harry ignored himself in the mirror and tried to think about what to wear.

Still Harry couldn't stop thinking about what he had done to that utterly gorgeous Brad ten years ago. Harry's hands started to sweat and his face started to turn red.

He knew straight away that he felt weird and a bit lightheaded. But he knew why after listening to all of his old school *friends* talk about how they felt with their girlfriends. He knew he was excited and happy to see Brad again.

Forcing himself up so he sat up on his soft, cool bed, Harry smiled as he was determined to do something about ten years ago. He might not be able to change the past, but he could easily change the future and make sure Brad wasn't the one who got away.

***

Standing outside the posh and extremely expensive looking hotel in the heart of London, Brad couldn't believe how amazing and posh it looked. A boy from Dover could never have imagined something like this.

The entire hotel was covered in beautiful clean glass at the front with everything inside that Brad could see covered in gold or some posh fabric. This was very posh.

Judging by all the expensive cars and black cabs running their engines and hearing the typical tip-tap of high heels, Brad knew everyone coming here worked in some high paid job.

From what Brad could remember of Harry's business card it mentioned something about accounting. Brad gave a silly little smile as he remembered that. It made Brad happy Harry had stuck to what he loved and wanted to do. Ever since they were 16 Harry had wanted to be an accountant. Brad was glad he achieved his dream.

Breathing in all the different smells of the poshly dressed people walking into the hotel with hints of flowers, earthy pine and manly scents hitting Brad left, right and centre. Brad started to wonder how beautiful Harry would look tonight.

Then his heart started to beat slightly faster as Brad wondered if his tight black slightly shiny suit would be okay. He hoped Harry would like it, but what if he didn't? What if Brad blew this?

That simple question made Brad cock his head briefly and smile, he needed to relax a little and admit something to himself. He needed to admit he still loved Harry. After all these years and lots of other relationships, Brad finally admitted he never really got over Harry. The amazing, sexy, beautiful boy from school that kissed him and left. The one that got away.

Brad kept smiling as he thought about it. That would explain why he never fully committed to a relationship. Of course it was silly but Brad had been given the chance to get with Harry. And he fully intended to take it.

A massive whiff of a strongly flowery perfume went up his nose as a posh elderly woman walked past.

After a few moments of watching more people walk past into the hotel, Brad's stomach turned into a knot or two at the idea of Harry not showing up. He had to turn up to his own work function, right?

Brad frowned as he thought Harry might pull a sicky or something and leave him again. Brad didn't want that. He wanted Harry, but he had no idea if Harry had accepted himself yet. What if he was still too scared to be gay? What if his work friends didn't know he was gay?

Those questions alone terrified him.

A small part of him wanted Brad to turn around and not come back here. Brad couldn't be hurt again.

Then Brad felt a soft, warm hand grab his and pulled him close. Brad's mouth dropped open as he was shocked by how beautiful Harry looked in his tight well-fitting grey suit. (That highlighted all the right places and his slightly muscular body)

Brad wrapped his arm around Harry's waist and as the two men walked into the stunning hotel, and

Brad felt light and filled with bliss. He knew Harry was right for him, and he thankfully wasn't the one who got away.

About the author:

Connor Whiteley is the author of over 40 books in the sci-fi fantasy, romance, nonfiction psychology and books for writer's genre.

He is a passionate warhammer 40,000 reader, psychology student and author.

Who narrates his own audiobooks and he hosts The Psychology World Podcast.

All whilst studying Psychology at the University of Kent, England.

Also, he was a former Explorer Scout where he gave a speech to the Maltese President in August 2018 and he attended Prince Charles' 70th Birthday Party at Buckingham Palace in May 2018.

Plus, he is a self-confessed coffee lover!

Gay Romance Short Stories:

Round The Parks and Beyond

Heart Around the Stones

Memorable Night

Love in Halls

The One That Got Away

Gay Romance Collection

Other books by Connor Whiteley:

The Fireheart Fantasy Series

Heart of Fire

Heart of Lies

More Coming Soon!

The Garro Series- Fantasy/Sci-fi

GARRO: GALAXY'S END

GARRO: RISE OF THE ORDER

GARRO: END TIMES

GARRO: SHORT STORIES

GARRO: COLLECTION

GARRO: HERESY

GARRO: FAITHLESS

GARRO: DESTROYER OF WORLDS

GARRO: COLLECTIONS BOOK 4-6

GARRO: MISTRESS OF BLOOD

GARRO: BEACON OF HOPE

GARRO: END OF DAYS

Winter Series- Fantasy Trilogy Books

WINTER'S COMING

WINTER'S HUNT

WINTER'S REVENGE

WINTER'S DISSENSION

Miscellaneous:

THE ANGEL OF RETURN

THE ANGEL OF FREEDOM

GAY ROMANCE COLLECTION

All books in 'An Introductory Series':

BIOLOGICAL PSYCHOLOGY 3RD EDITION

COGNITIVE PSYCHOLOGY THIRD EDITION

SOCIAL PSYCHOLOGY- 3RD EDITION

ABNORMAL PSYCHOLOGY 3RD EDITION

PSYCHOLOGY OF RELATIONSHIPS- 3RD EDITION

DEVELOPMENTAL PSYCHOLOGY 3RD EDITION

HEALTH PSYCHOLOGY

RESEARCH IN PSYCHOLOGY

A GUIDE TO MENTAL HEALTH AND TREATMENT AROUND THE WORLD- A GLOBAL LOOK AT DEPRESSION

FORENSIC PSYCHOLOGY

THE FORENSIC PSYCHOLOGY OF THEFT, BURGLARY AND OTHER RIMES AGAINST PROPERTY

CRIMINAL PROFILING: A FORENSIC PSYCHOLOGY GUIDE TO FBI PROFILING AND GEOGRAPHICAL AND STATISTICAL PROFILING.

CLINICAL PSYCHOLOGY

FORMULATION IN PSYCHOTHERAPY

PERSONALITY PSYCHOLOGY AND INDIVIDUAL DIFFERENCES

CLINICAL PSYCHOLOGY REFLECTIONS VOLUME 1

CLINICAL PSYCHOLOGY REFLECTIONS VOLUME 2

www.ingramcontent.com/pod-product-compliance
Lightning Source LLC
LaVergne TN
LVHW011853060526
838200LV00054B/4311